GHOST TOWN

A Novel

GHOST TOWN

A Novel

✢ Noah Lane ✢

Ghost Town

Copyright © 2025 Noah Lane

All rights reserved. No part of this publication may be reproduced, stored in any retrieval system, or transmitted in any form or by any means, mechanical, photocopying, recording, or otherwise, without permission in writing from the publisher, except by a reviewer, who may quote brief passages in a review.

This is a work of fiction. All of the characters, organizations, and events portrayed in this novel are either products of the author's imagination or are used fictitiously.

Cover and Interior design by Ted Ruybal
100% Human Made. No AI Editing Used.

Manufactured in the United States of America

Wisdom House Books
For more information, please contact:
www.wisdomhousebooks.com

Paperback ISBN: 979-8-9912462-0-0
LCCN: 2025903161

FIC009100 | FICTION / Fantasy / Action & Adventure
FIC022000 | FICTION / Mystery & Detective / General
YAF001000 | YOUNG ADULT FICTION / Action & Adventure / General

1 2 3 4 5 6 7 8 9 10
First Edition 2025

Table of Contents

Chapter One 1

Chapter Two 9

Chapter Three 17

Chapter Four 29

Chapter Five 45

Chapter Six 55

Chapter Seven 67

Chapter Eight 75

Chapter Nine 87

About the Author 105

Chapter One

Bang! Bang! Bang! The sound of my hammer smashed against the forge. It was late at night and my boss Captain Dust, had ordered me to make all kinds of weapons for the trip across seas tomorrow.

My name is Thomas Yearwood. For a while now, my life has been really screwed up. I used to have a family like everyone else, but one day I was separated from them—presumably for life. Since then, I have been living as a slave under the control of Captain Dust. I still find myself thinking about my family—my beautiful wife Olivia, with her blonde hair and blue eyes, and our son, Issac. I myself have brown messy hair, brown eyes, and am very tan and tall. I didn't used to be so tan but because of all the time working out in the sun my skin stays tan year-round. I remember Issac used to look exactly like me when I was his age.

It all happened so fast. The year was 1945. Captain

Ghost Town

Dust and his crew ravaged our town. There was a major fight that broke out. Captain Dust took me hostage since I was a strong man who hadn't left for war. He shipped me overseas, and then I was here. I live in Europe, more specifically the UK. I and the other slaves are all under the control of Captain Dust. But I'm not like the other slaves. Most of them are much younger than me and are single men. I had a family.

Captain Dust is hard on us. He doesn't show much mercy with bombarding us with work. I have frequently found myself working late into the night hours. I wouldn't call myself one of Captain Dust's favorite slaves but I'm definitely not his least favorite. There is some trust involved since he trusts me enough to work in the forge.

After hours of work, I finally finished making all the weapons for tomorrow. I stepped outside and the cold air greeted me. I went over towards the lake that surrounded our camp. I sat down and looked at my reflection. It stared back at me. Tomorrow we will be crossing the sea to America. Suddenly a feeling of hope rose up in my chest. I hadn't felt this feeling in such a long time. In fact, I hadn't felt that feeling in . . . ten years. *I have been a slave for ten years.* The reality hit me like a brick. Has it really been that long? It felt like it had only been one or two years. It was now 1955.

Chapter One

I wondered how Issac had grown over this time. If only I could see him.

I decided now would be a good time to try and get some sleep. It had to be well past midnight, and I needed sleep to be ready for tomorrow. I tossed and turned but found it impossible to fall asleep.

Eventually morning came, and I heard Eric, a fellow slave, banging on the doors to wake people up. He was charged with this annoying task each morning. Groggily, I got out of bed and headed into breakfast with all the other slaves in our camp. After breakfast, we walked the three miles where our ship sat nestled against the dock. They had been building that ship for over a year getting ready for this day. The ship was a massive old pirate-like ship that was extremely old-fashioned than what most people would use nowadays. A rusted old green steering wheel stood silently at the front of the ship. No doubt it could steer the ship, but the color of the wheel made me wonder.

"Thomas!" Captain Dust's words shook me. "Did you finish making the weapons?"

"Yes sir," I said.

"Good. Since you won't be working the forge while we're at sea, your new job will be doing maintenance on the ship. You'll be making sure there aren't any leaks, cleaning the floors, that type of stuff," he said.

I sighed on the inside. I would rather work the forge any day than be stuck doing maintenance.

"Now get to work," Dust said.

"Yes sir," I replied, biting my tongue.

I hurried off the dock and helped other slaves load cargo onto the ship. Planning a trip like this in the middle of winter made many slaves skeptical of Captain Dust, but no one wanted to stand up and tell him that this made no sense if we ran into any kind of bad weather. *Not even me*, I thought.

Eventually when all the work was done, everyone started piling onto the ship. The ship snapped against the mooring ropes as I stepped onboard last. We had set sail.

Over the next two weeks the boat sailed through endless ocean. I had plenty of tasks to keep me busy, but time seemed to move in slow motion. Finally, the last day of travel came. Word passed through the slaves that the ship had nearly reached America. Just maybe, I was going to see my family again.

That night a series of crashing sounds blasted me out of a deep sleep. It had to be past midnight. What was going on? Multiple people in the room were getting out of their beds. Part of the ship was leaking. Water was spilling into

Chapter One

the bottom floor where we slept.

"What's happening?" I frantically asked.

"Bad storm, I don't know how we're going to make it out of this one," said one of the slaves.

I pushed my way past people into the other room. The ship started to rock. Everyone was yelling and panicking. Water was flooding the bottom floor. I jumped and grabbed a railing and watched as everyone clamored to stay above the rushing water. Higher and higher I climbed up the ship as I began to hear claps of thunder. I burst through the door to the deck of the ship and realized what was going on. We were in the middle of a storm. A massive one. It looked like a hurricane mixed with a tornado and I looked above me as massive dark clouds swirled in the sky. The ship was sinking. I ran over to the lifeboats where multiple others were. It looked like I was too late. Captain Dust was deploying the last lifeboat.

"Captain Dust, wait!" I shouted. "You've got to let me on that lifeboat! Please!" I begged.

"Why would I do that Thomas? Do you not see all the others asking for the same thing?"

"Yes, but there's one seat left, and besides, who would work the forge if I was gone?"

"The lifeboat is full." Captain Dust said coldly as he

shifted his body to take up two seats.

"I've done everything you've ever asked!" I pleaded to him.

I suddenly became very angry which was rare for me.

"I've taken all your orders without a single complaint and you're just going to leave me to die? I have a family. I need to find them!"

"You have a family?" Dust mocked. "So, did I. And guess where they are now? They're gone! But I didn't sit there, I moved on! I never should have trusted you with the forge."

I watched in horror as Captain Dust cut the rope deploying the last lifeboat stranding me on this sinking ship. He eventually faded off into the distance along with the lifeboat. I kept thinking about the last thing he said to me. *I never should have trusted you with the forge.*

The rain felt like bullets as it hit my face. Not to my skin, but to my heart. Those words stung me. Even though I knew Captain Dust wasn't a great person, I had worked countless hours in the forge, and after all this time he showed no respect for me. That pushed me over the edge, and I felt extremely defeated. The storm didn't look like it was going to stop anytime soon either. Half an hour or so more and this ship would be completely submerged. I ran

Chapter One

to the deck station and stopped cold looking at the empty old green steering wheel standing silently at the helm. The helmsman had vanished—or perhaps drowned.

I quickly realized I had two choices, I could either try and pilot the wheel to this sinking ship—even though I didn't know how far away shore might be, nor whether I could steer the ship—or I could . . . jump. I shuddered at the thought of the latter. It's the middle of winter! The water's probably freezing! I looked down into the choppy water, and the thought of jumping seemed more and more tempting. Every second that slipped away the ship listed more and more towards its side. I made up my mind. I was going to jump even if it killed me. I took one last look at the sinking pirate ship and then plunged into the ice-cold water. The water slammed against my body; it was much colder than I had imagined. My skin seared in pain. I knew if I didn't get out of the water soon, I was going to get hypothermia. The storm made swimming impossible as I got carried further and further away from the ship by the waves. I blacked out.

Chapter Two

I opened my eyes but immediately closed them due to the blinding sun. I had bruises all over my body. Dry land and sea walls surrounded me. Where am I? I was alive at least; the waves must have carried me to the shore. Dazed, I got up from the wet sand and walked a few hundred yards down the shoreline where I came to a beach packed with people.

"Um, excuse me," I asked a man, who was relaxing in the winter sun, which was shockingly warm for this time of year. "Where am I?"

"Oh, you are in Virginia." the man said.

Virginia? I made it. *I was in America.* I thought.

I walked around lost for the next hour. I had not been in America for ten years. The reality of the situation crashed down upon me like a wave. Excitement and fear flooded my mind. Where was I going to go? What was I

Ghost Town

going to do? I had no money on me, no supplies, and no shelter. I was so used to having all that stuff provided for me. No, I'll be fine, I told myself. I'm in my home state after all. My family's probably here—I need to find them.

I need to get off this beach. My clothes were all torn up and my face was covered in dirt and grime. It felt much warmer here than in the UK and it was a clear sunny day. It had been weeks since I had seen sunlight. It's always so dark and gray in the UK that the sun was a nice refresher. Suddenly, I had a flashback to last night. Where was everyone now? I hoped that most of them made it out alive. Where was Captain Dust? I doubted I'd ever find the answers to my questions. I had lived with some of those people for a decade. And now I didn't think I would see any of them again. For some reason, I felt sad. Slavery was all I had left, but now that was gone.

I walked until I came off the beach and onto solid land. I didn't have a plan for where I was going. I was just wandering around. I walked into a neighborhood full of beach houses and near the front of it, I saw a rough drawn map, hanging from a tree. That's when it hit me.

My best friend, Robert Jones, once had a beach house near here. I had gone to college with Robert, and he was the best man at my wedding. My thoughts made me yearn

Chapter Two

for the past.

Doubts immediately flooded my mind. He probably doesn't even own the house anymore. After all, it's been ten years. But the prospect of seeing Robert was too great to keep me down. I remembered hanging out on this beach for hours at a time, and now I recalled exactly what his house looked like. It was flat roofed with neat, widely framed windows. After walking for a while I found the house. It was the third street back from the beach. I stepped up to the door of the house—and with a deep breath, I rang the doorbell.

"Robert, there's someone at the door," said a female voice I didn't recognize.

"I'll get it," Robert said.

He opened the door and as soon as he recognized me he dropped the coffee mug that was in his hand as it fell to the doormat, shattering.

"Thomas?" Robert asked. "Is it really you? After all this time?"

"Yeah, it's me," I said awkwardly.

"I . . . I thought you were dead," said Robert.

"It's a long story." I said.

"Okay, well you can come inside and tell me about it," Robert said as he picked up the shattered pieces of his coffee mug.

I stepped up to the door and was shocked to find that the inside of his beach house was sparkling clean. In the past when Robert was my roommate in college his room was always super messy. This was not who I remembered. He seemed more mature now, less sporadic. Like me, Robert had brown hair but his was shaggier than mine, and he had blue eyes versus my brown ones.

"Thomas, what happened to you?" Robert said, taking note of my torn clothes and bruised body."

"It's been a long day." I said. "I'm exhausted."

"Then we can talk later," said Robert. "There's an extra shower that none of us are using so you can use it and get cleaned up. I have some extra clothes of mine that you can wear as well."

"Us?" I asked.

"Oh yeah, I'm married now. Robert said nonchalantly."

Robert extended his left hand to show a ring. A woman suddenly walked through the house. She had shiny dark brown hair which was tied in a ponytail.

"Mia, meet Thomas," Robert said.

I was shocked by the fact that Robert had a wife. I shouldn't have been, I mean he was the same age as me,

Chapter Two

but I had always imagined Robert single. Robert was never really into girls when I met him in college and people even joked that he would never get married.

"Oh, hello," Mia said to me.

Suddenly, a small girl came flying into the living room with a box of crayons in her hand.

"Oh, yeah—forgot to add, I also have a kid now," said Robert. "This is Emma."

Emma looked like a perfect mix between Robert and Mia. She had the eyes and hair of Mia, but she looked determined—a trait that Robert embodied.

"How old is she?" I asked.

"She is about to turn six. She's in kindergarten." said Mia.

"Say hi Thomas," Robert instructed Emma.

"Hi Thomas," Emma said quietly.

"Well, I should probably go shower," I said.

"Oh yeah, go right ahead," said Robert.

A hot clean shower felt amazing. Yesterday, I would have had five minutes to take a freezing one.

After I showered, I came back into the living room and Robert offered me some food to eat. I never realized the depth of my hunger until I took the first bite of bread he gave me. I settled down across from Robert on the

Ghost Town

couch and began telling him about how I had arrived here. I told him everything that had happened since I last saw him—getting shipped to Europe, being under Captain Dust's control and then escaping by jumping off the sinking ship.

"Wow," said Robert. "I didn't realize how easy I had it here with my family. I'm sorry about what happened to you."

A sudden feeling of homesickness ran down my spine.

"I'm so glad you found me because I thought I'd never see you again." said Robert.

"Yeah, well, I'm glad to have a friend like you." I said. "Can I ask you a question? Why are you visiting the beach now?" I thought you wouldn't be here; it's winter after all." I questioned.

"Well, we didn't get to go to the beach this summer and Emma has been dying to go, so we told her we'd take her this winter—and so far, it hasn't been too cold." said Robert.

The conversation then shifted to Robert talking about how he met Mia, then it shifted back to me.

"Well, since it appears you've escaped slavery, why not stay here for a while? We have an extra bed near the back of the house. You're free now, after all." explained Robert.

Chapter Two

"Yeah, I am *free*." I said. "But I can't stay here. I need to find my family."

"Oh," said Robert grimly. "They moved away. I lost contact with Olivia years ago"

"What?" I asked, panic rising in my chest. "Do you know where they are now?"

"Well yeah, they moved to California, but that's a long way from here." said Robert.

"Ok, well I need to find them. I can book a train or maybe drive a car there or something."

"Look Thomas, I don't know if your family is still . . . I don't know if they're still there." said Robert.

"Well, I have to try at least." I said.

"Thomas, I know you want to find your family. And I know you're hurt. But that's a faraway place to go right now. Plus, do you even have any money?"

"No," I said disappointingly.

"You just escaped slavery! Don't you feel free? Tomorrow we were thinking of going to the beach. Why don't you come with us and relax a bit?" said Robert.

"How am I supposed to relax when my family is out there, and they could be in danger? My son is growing up without a father! And I want to be there for him. I would rather die than lose my family again."

Ghost Town

Robert went quiet and the atmosphere tensed up. After a while, he spoke up.

"I understand," he said. "If I was in your situation I'd want the same thing. Tell you what, tomorrow we can drive back to my main house and from there we can take a train from Virginia to California."

"I thought you wanted to go to the beach tomorrow." I said.

"Well, you seeing your family is much more important," he said.

"You mean it?" I asked.

"Of course, said Robert. "Also, don't worry about the money. I've got that covered. Maybe you should take up my idea of going to the beach this afternoon. I've got to go take Emma to art camp, so I'll talk to you later."

"Thank you." I said.

Robert turned and explained the situation to Mia. Mia agreed then told me she felt so sorry for what had happened to me. I decided to go to the beach later that day. I was free. Things were finally looking up for me. I hadn't felt this hopeful in years.

Chapter Three

I woke up the next morning super early. I guess I was so used to getting up early from working the forge as a slave that I didn't even notice I was the first one up. Once Robert and Mia woke up, I helped pack things into their car for the drive home. Robert had a nice black pickup truck. I thanked them multiple times, but Robert said it wasn't a big deal since they were going to leave in a few days anyway. Robert seemed quite relaxed while driving—having only one hand on the wheel. As we traveled, he and Mia told me what had happened while I was gone. They explained how World War II had ended, and peace had been restored to the country. I was just now starting to realize how much of my life I had missed.

The drive flew by in the blink of an eye as Robert's truck ran down the highway. This whole day still felt like one big dream. I was half expecting to have woken

Ghost Town

up back at the camp in slavery. Eventually we arrived at Robert's house. It was a small gray house with big windows and a spacious front yard. The roof was angular, and the view was beautiful. Robert had a nice location of not living in a city but still being very close to one. Mia put Emma down for a nap while Robert and I unloaded everything from his truck. Once we were inside Robert grabbed three handfuls of one-hundred-dollar bills and put them in a duffel bag. Robert guided me to his closet and picked out three days of clothes that we could each wear. He said that it would take us three days to get to California from Virginia. We would stay at a hotel for two nights and then get there on the third day. Traveling by a train would be our best bet.

"You ready, Thomas?" Robert said as we both finished packing the items we had taken from the closet into two nearly identical black suitcases.

"Bye Robert," said Mia as she kissed him on the cheek. "Good luck Thomas. Tell me if you find them."

"I will," I said.

As Robert and I walked to the train station, I noticed that the weather was quite strange. It was super foggy out, yet bits of sunlight poked through the clouds. Light rain poured down from above. Once we arrived, I saw that

Chapter Three

the train was a dark sea green color which reminded me of the color of the wheel of Captain Dust's ship. *Weird.* I thought.

The steam powered train looked elegant as the morning sun glistened off its windows. A crowd of passengers filled the station. We were on time, yet we were one of the last people to board the train.

"Tickets?" asked the conductor.

"Here you go," I said as I handed our tickets to the conductor.

"Have a great ride," said the conductor.

Robert and I agreed I would use a fake last name to prevent me from being identified as a slave. I came up with the idea for the last name of Adams simply because I thought it sounded cool. We found our way to the last row of seats at the end of the passenger car. We had a long train ride ahead of us. Fatigue overtook me as I settled into my seat and extended my legs under the seat in front of me. I was surprised that Robert spent this much money on such a nice train just to accompany me to see my family. But nonetheless I was grateful. As the train sped along its path, I began to learn more and more about who Robert was. He appeared much different than he was ten years ago, and I felt a tiny bit disconnected from him.

Ghost Town

The man I spent several years hanging out with wasn't exactly the man that I was talking to right now.

About an hour later I saw several passengers looking out their window—seeming very confused.

"Hey, Robert shouldn't the train have stopped back there?" I asked.

"It's probably fine," he said. "Just trust the conductor."

"Are you sure? I may go check with him to make sure everything is going ok. The last thing I want happening is the train missing our stop." I said.

"Ok," said Robert. "But we're right on schedule."

"I'm just going to make sure." I said.

I walked all the way to the front of the train and said; "Um excuse me, I was wondering if the train should have . . ."

I stopped mid-sentence. I stared at the place where the conductor or engineer should have been driving the train, but the seat sat empty. My heart skipped a beat. *Who was driving the train?* I asked myself.

Suddenly, the train swerved right off the tracks. Oh no, I thought. The train is off the tracks. And it's going straight through a city! Up ahead, what looked to be a solid row of four-story buildings stood in the way.

What do I do? I asked myself.

Just then, I saw someone walking into the front compartment through the breezeway.

Chapter Three

"Everything ok up here?" Robert asked.

I then saw the blank look on his face as he stared into the empty control room.

"Where's the conductor?" asked Robert, his voice level raising.

"How am I supposed to know?" I snapped back.

The train swerved left this time, and I began hearing shouts from people in the back wondering what was going on. With every passing second the train was inching closer and closer to crashing into those buildings.

"Here, you steer the train, I'll deal with the passengers," said Robert.

"I've never driven a train before!" I shouted.

"Can you at least try?" pleaded Robert.

Hordes of people were trying to see what was going on as Robert tried to console them that everything was going to be ok. I gripped the throttle of the train. The train started to accelerate closer to the buildings.

"Why are we going faster?" Robert yelled at me.

"I don't know how to pilot this thing!" I shouted back.

I needed to find the brakes. My eyes scanned the area, and I saw what looked to be a brake lever. I grabbed it and pulled on it with all my strength. The train started to slow down and screech to a halt, but it wasn't enough. Then I

Ghost Town

watched as the train crashed straight into three four story buildings.

The train sputtered and coughed and finally came to a complete stop. Smoke filled the air while the scream of a siren pierced my ears. People started to scramble to get out of the crowded train. I needed to get my bearings to know what to do next.

"Everyone ok?" asked Robert.

In the distance I could hear police sirens going off.

"Oh great, the police are here," muttered Robert.

The fire department, police, and ambulance all shortly arrived at the scene. Eight police officers came through the wrecked train and inspected the crash site.

One of the police officers came directly to the damaged front compartment. He towered over me—and I'm pretty tall myself so that's saying something. His demeanor reminded me of someone.

"You! Can you tell me exactly what the heck is going on here? A runaway train? Where's the conductor? And why did you think that it was a good idea to steer the train? Why didn't you ask the head engineer?"

"You saw me steering the train?" I asked.

"Yeah, and maybe if you had better driving skills then maybe this train wouldn't have crashed!" his voice level

Chapter Three

raised on the last word.

I always hated the police. I always thought they had too much authority on their hands, but this was taking it to a new level.

"I'm sorry, who exactly are you?" I interjected.

"My name is Officer Rhyder Ashdown." He pointed a finger at his badge on his chest. "Who are you?"

"My name is Thomas Adams." I shrugged.

At that moment Robert entered the room.

"And who are you? Thomas's main accomplice?" Ashdown asked Robert.

Accomplice? Who does he think I am, some kind of criminal? I thought.

"I'm Robert Jones, Thomas is with me. Officer, I can tell you exactly what happened. Thomas and I boarded the train like normal with plans of making our way to California to visit Thomas's family. Thomas decided to go and ask the conductor to make sure the train wasn't missing any stops; however, when he got up there the conductor was nowhere to be found leaving the train with no one driving it."

"So, what, the conductor just disappeared?" said Ashdown. "I don't buy it. Where did he go?"

"We don't know," I said.

"Well, you two have got a lot of nerve piloting a runaway

train. You've caused a lot of damage to the city and I'm afraid I'm going to have to give you a fine of three-hundred thousand dollars' worth of property destruction."

"Whoa, whoa, whoa," Robert snapped back. "Before you start giving out fines don't you think it's a good idea to check if everyone is ok?"

"Already did that," said Ashdown. "My other officers did that. No deaths but a few injuries."

I suddenly felt very guilty.

"Well sir, a lot of our money got destroyed in the train crash. We share money. We're uh, brothers." I said.

"Well, you still drove a train illegally, destroyed the train, and part of these buildings. I'm afraid I still have to give you the fine." said Ashdown.

"So, what was I supposed to do, just let the train go off on its own and cause even more damage?" I was trying to stop it from hitting the buildings!" I said angrily.

"Well then you didn't do a very good job, did you?" Ashdown remarked.

Robert sighed.

"Look Officer, we don't have that kind of money right now."

"Then you will have to take on a significant burden of debt. I'll give you one month to pay it off." he said.

Chapter Three

"Only one month?" said Robert, horrified.

"That's all I can do for you," he said, although I suspected he was lying.

"And what if we don't pay it off in a month?" I asked, knowing the answer.

"Well then, you'll go to jail," said Ashdown.

"For how long?" I asked.

"Probably around ten years."

There was a long pause before he spoke again.

"Here's my card. I'll be waiting for the money."

As he left the wreckage, we stood there not knowing what to do next. I followed Robert out of the crashed train. The sun had now been completely covered by clouds. The light rain had turned into heavy rain. The cold air cut right through my jacket. I kept following him for a while before I finally asked:

"Where exactly are we going?"

"Home," said Robert.

"But I thought we were going to see my family?"

"Yeah, well things have changed. We're now deep in debt."

"Look, it's not my fault. You were the one who told me to pilot the train!" I said.

"Did I blame you?" Robert's words were sharp. "We

Ghost Town

have no money. Our money was destroyed in the train crash. I have no idea how we are going to pay off that debt in one month. I need your help. If we don't pay this off, we are going to go to jail. I need you to get a job."

I wanted to argue back but the words just wouldn't come out of my mouth.

"I understand." I finally said, feeling defeated.

Despite what I told Robert, I felt like this was my whole fault. If I had just let someone else take the wheel to the train, then maybe things wouldn't have gone this way. I had a sinking feeling that it was going to be a while before I was going to get to see my family.

Robert used the little money that he had in his pocket to buy us a bus ticket home. We arrived just before dusk. What a day, I thought. I still couldn't get that feeling out of the pit of my stomach that things were only going to get worse from here. That the train crash was just the beginning.

We unpacked the luggage from Robert's truck and greeted Emma and Mia. Emma was stoked to see Robert, but I could tell Mia was worried. Robert explained to her the situation.

"So, the train conductor just disappeared? What happened to him? And what's Thomas going to do?" asked

Chapter Three

Mia anxiously.

"Well, I was thinking Thomas could stay with us for a little while and get a job. He could help us pay off the debt," said Robert.

He then pulled Mia aside. "Look I know this is hard, and I know we don't make enough money to pay off this kind of debt. But I promise you, I'm not going to spend the next ten years behind bars."

That night, I lay in bed awake. Every time I tried to drift off to sleep my thoughts would keep me awake. I overheard Robert and Mia having a conversation in the other room.

"Robert, do you think that Thomas is ok?" asked Mia.

"Thomas? Yeah, he's good, he's just been through a lot—more than I have in fact. It's just sometimes I wonder if he seems a little . . ."

"Too optimistic?" said Mia.

"Yeah." said Robert. "I mean I hate to break it to him, but I don't know if his family is even still alive. I stopped talking to Oliva years ago, and people change, and I don't think Thomas gets that. I'm not the same man I was ten years ago, and neither is he. I wonder what would happen if he found out that they're gone. I just think that him wanting to find his family so bad is a distraction from the pain and trauma he endured while he was a slave. But he's a good man. We need to help him out."

"We will." said Mia.

"Goodnight hon," said Robert.

"Night," said Mia.

I didn't know whether to feel insulted or complimented by what Robert was saying. But if he had been in slavery for ten years, wouldn't he want to see his family too? I just didn't understand. I *knew* that my family was out there somewhere. I could feel it. He could call it blind optimism, but what I liked to call it, was hope. That thought finally allowed me to drift off to sleep.

Chapter Four

I woke up early again the next morning. Robert's coffee machine was out in the open ready to make me a cup of fresh coffee to jolt me out of my exhaustion. All I wanted to do was go back to bed but my internal clock told me otherwise. I decided since I was already up, I should go for a walk. As I stepped out the door, I glanced at the red thermometer hanging on the post just beyond the step. I leaned closer to see it read thirty degrees. The weather had certainly taken a turn. It was hard to believe a few days ago, I was out on the beach in the sun.

After an easy twenty-five-minute walk in the brisk morning air, I stepped back on Robert and Mia's front step. I laid my jacket down next to the front door and took a few steps back to the kitchen where Robert sat reading something at the table and Mia facing the counter near the sink. I forgot. Today was a workday so Robert had to go to work. I'd learned that Robert was an architect, and Mia was a stay-at-home mom.

"Hey, Thomas, have you looked for a job yet?" asked Robert.

"No, I haven't had any time," I said. "Plus, I don't know how I'm supposed to find a job that I actually enjoy. I mean it's been ten years since I last worked."

"Why don't you look in the newspaper?" Robert said, as he pointed down to the employment section of the newspaper, which was lying on the table. "That thing is usually full of advertisements for jobs."

"I guess I could try that." I shrugged.

Mia stopped whatever she had been working on at the sink and helped me put together a bowl of oatmeal to have for breakfast. While eating, I skimmed through the newspaper when something caught my eye.

"What's that?" asked Robert, peering over my shoulder.

"It's an ad for a job at a detective company called *Foglight Investigations*." I said.

"A detective company?" Robert asked, surprised.

"Yeah, it says: *Our company is dedicated to solving mysteries and crimes. No prior experience needed. The only requirement is that you must be eighteen years or older.*

Doesn't really go into specifics, I thought.

Chapter Four

"That job sounds like it suits you," Robert said. "You'd make a great detective."

"You think so?" I said, skeptical.

"Of course. Where's it located anyway?" asked Robert.

"It says here it's located near the back of a street called Bishops Circle."

"Oh, that's got to be at least ten miles from here." said Robert. "I guess you can use my old car if you want to check the place out. The keys are on the hook in the kitchen. I think you should go there."

"I guess I could do that today." I said.

"Ok, well I need to get to work. I hope you're able get an interview—and if you do, I hope it goes well." said Robert.

"Thanks," I said.

After Robert left for work and Mia left to take Emma to school, I pulled out a map and grabbed Robert's light gray jacket he said I could use. I grabbed the car keys and headed out to the garage. That's where I found Robert's old gray car. You could tell the age of the car as the paint was rusted and it had scratches all over it. Despite its old age, it was better than nothing. I opened the door to the car, inserted the key and the engine started. That's when I realized that I hadn't driven a car in ten years. Did I even remember how to? It didn't help that the car I was driving was super old and probably had a lot of issues that needed to be fixed.

As I reversed out of the garage memories of long ago when I first learned how to drive flooded my mind. The car creaked and the tires squirmed while I was pulling out. This car clearly had not been driven in years. But soon enough I was in the flow of traffic and I started to get the hang of driving a little more. I took out the map Robert gave me and navigated my way to the proper street.

Directly across Bishops Circle I was able to find a parking spot for this run-down car. I parked it right behind a nice white van and got out of the car. The building I came to was not at all what I was expecting. It was a tall and narrow gray building located at the very back of the street. Most of the windows were black and the atmosphere was not at all welcoming. *What have I gotten myself into?* I thought.

I opened the broad, navy-blue doors, and stepped inside the building. It was just as cramped on the inside as it was on the outside. There was only one person in the main room. It was a woman who looked to be in her late twenties or early thirties. She wore dark green glasses and

Chapter Four

had long dark brown hair. She appeared to be quite bored.

"Um, hi, I'm here to inquire about a possible interview for the detective job you are offering. I read about you guys in this morning's paper. My name is Thomas Adams." I said.

After a long period of silence, the woman responded and said; "You know, you're the first person in a while to apply for this job."

That didn't exactly calm my nerves. I saw good reason why people wouldn't want to come to a dingy detective place at the back of a street, but desperate times call for desperate measures.

"My name is Elizabeth West." the woman said. "I am the co-manager of our detective company. I am also the one who wrote the ad in the paper. As of right now we are at a lack of staff, so I'm having to run both the front desk and the interviews. Do you have any prior detective experience?" she asked me.

"Um, no, I don't have any," I said. "But the paper said I didn't need any."

"Hmph, well then, you'll need to meet with Atlas. Atlas Cooper. He's the founder of the company. I only interview the candidates with prior experience. Atlas might seem a little brash, but he's been through a lot.

Ghost Town

Come with me."

Elizibeth directed me all the way up to the third story of the building. The second story had a few people—who looked hard at work trying to figure out a case. One of them was sorting something. The other was looking through folders with people's names on them. I was surprised at how messy this place was. At the third story Elizibeth knocked on a large brown door.

"This leads to Atlas's office." she told me.

"Who is it?" grumbled a voice that came from the other side of the door.

"It's Elizabeth, and I want you to meet a possible recruit, Thomas Adams. He says that as of right now he doesn't have any detective experience but that can change."

"Come in," Atlas said quietly. "Just Thomas."

Elizabeth gave me an approving look as she walked back down the stairs. I slowly opened the large door and found myself standing in front of Atlas. He was tall and had a huge frame. He was wearing all black clothing and some type of uniform. His hair was mostly black with some gray dispersed throughout. I looked him in the eyes. He wore grief on his face. His office was littered with several wine bottles on top of a bookcase. It was a dark and gloomy place with many shades of brown, gray, and black.

Chapter Four

"So, what exactly makes you think you'd be a good detective?" Atlas asked me.

"Well," I said, slightly nervous. "I have a knack for problem solving and I need to make some money. I'm not from around here." I bit my tongue.

What if he finds out I was a slave? This is the last guy I would want to find out that information.

"Then where are you from?" he asked me.

"California." I said, seeing no reason to lie since that would only raise suspicion.

"What are you doing all the way over here in Virginia?" asked Atlas gruffly.

"It's a long story." I said. "I have a family back in California, but I don't have enough money to travel there."

Atlas's eyes suddenly went soft, and his tough persona vanished. "I once had a family too."

A second later his eyes went back to normal, and his seriousness came back to him.

"Here's the thing," he said. "A bunch of cases of missing people have been filed across the state. In fact, an alarming rate of missing people. I haven't had this many cases to go through and this few staff since, well since . . ." His voice trailed off.

"Look, today I'll work with you on the basics of being

a detective." Atlas said. "Tomorrow, I will give you your first mission. Here's a case of a young couple who reported their daughter missing. I want you to drive over to their house and figure out what happened to her. Do you think you're up for the task?"

"Yes sir," I said.

"Good, cause you're hired. It's time for me to teach you what it means to be a real detective." Atlas explained.

Over the next few hours Atlas taught what it meant to be a detective. He showed me many cases that he had done in the past and he led me downstairs where I got to meet Jerimiah and Drake, who were technically my co-workers. He told me things that I never would have thought to do. Atlas's teaching was interesting. He seemed very strict and tough, but at the end of the day, I felt like he cared for me. I wondered what happened to his family. That evening, Atlas even gave me my own badge that read *Foglight Investigations*. I stuck it onto my jacket. I expected to go home since it was getting dark outside, but it surprised me when he asked; "Thomas, you don't mind working a late first night, do you?"

"First night?" I asked. "I thought I wasn't going to start until tomorrow."

"Yeah well, I've decided since you've done well in

Chapter Four

training, It's time for your first mission. It's 8:30 pm right now, so I want you back in my office by midnight. I'm giving you four hours to complete this mission."

Shoot, I thought. Mia and Robert probably wouldn't appreciate me staying out so late.

"What's with the look on your face? Can you make it work or not?" asked Atlas.

"Yes, I can make it work," I said.

They'll get over it. I thought.

"Alright, the house is located on Enoch street," said Atlas. "Oh, and you might want this. Just in case." He handed me a shiny black pistol.

"Why would I need this?" I asked.

"Well, it's going to be dark. It's if you get attacked of course. Now, go out there and solve a mystery. Don't fail me, Thomas."

"I won't," I replied back.

I took the pistol from his hands. I was finally starting to feel like I was in control. I headed back out into the parking lot filled with energy to get this mission completed. But, somewhere deep inside me I knew that this wasn't the best idea.

As I drove, the streetlamps sparkled along the edges of the roadway in front of me. The headlights to Robert's

Ghost Town

old car flickered on and off as I strained to see the dark roads. I pulled out a map halfway through just to make sure I knew where I was going. Finally, after a sea full of traffic I made it to the right street. I quickly parked about ten feet from the bus stop sign on the curb, opened the door and that's when I heard something alarming.

I heard a trash can being knocked over. I walked closer to the noise. That's when I could make out the silhouette of two men who appeared to be in a fight in the alleyway. I took the pistol and gripped it in my hands.

"Hand over your wallet!" one of the men screamed at the other.

I aimed the pistol at the men.

"Step out of darkness and put your hands where I can see them." I directed. "Both of you."

A man wearing all black stepped out from the shadow of the alleyway. He looked extremely thin and sickly pale. The other man was lying on the ground in the alleyway still in the shadow.

"You're a cop?" asked the thief who had stepped out of the dark alley. "You certainly don't look like one." he laughed.

"I wouldn't be the one talking if I were you. I'm not the one with a gun pointed at me." I quickly snapped back.

Chapter Four

"Ok then go ahead. Pull the trigger. Shoot me. You won't . . ."

That response took me aback.

"What?"

"You heard me. If you really are that serious then pull the trigger and shoot me."

My hands tightened around the grip of the pistol. I didn't know what to do.

"You're weak," muttered the thief.

Part of me wanted to pull the trigger but I just didn't have it in me. I dropped the gun, and it fell to the ground.

The thief then retreated into the alley out of my field of vision. I rushed back into the alleyway to follow him. But when I got back there, it was empty. Where did he go? I looked down to see if I could find the other man who had been lying on the ground presumably knocked out by the thief. But again, I saw no one. They couldn't have escaped; it was a dead end. So, what happened? As if things couldn't get any worse suddenly a familiar voice hit me.

"Thomas? What are you doing back there? And why is the pistol I gave you lying on the ground? Are you asking to be shot?" called Atlas.

"No, sir I can explain . . ."

Ghost Town

"How many hours did I give you to do this mission?" Atlas demanded. His voice was sharp.

"Um, four sir." I said.

"And how many hours has it been?" asked Atlas.

"Well, it's been two."

"Exactly Thomas, what did you do? Get lost driving here in that beat up car? My office is not more than twenty-five minutes from here. When you weren't back in an hour I figured I'd better come see what had happened to you. And then I see that you decided to get yourself involved in a petty robbery." Atlas remarked.

I could tell that he was starting to get heated.

"Look, if you'll just listen then I can explain!" The anger burst out of me. I couldn't take much more of this.

"Ok fine, say what's on your mind, it better be worth it," muttered Atlas.

"I walked into this alley because I saw a criminal who was beating up an innocent man. I guess I thought naively that since I was armed, that I could . . . arrest him."

Saying it out loud sounded very dumb.

"Did you really think you would have the power to arrest someone when you don't even have a single mission under your belt? You're not even a police officer!" Atlas retorted.

Chapter Four

"Look I know . . ." I started to say before Atlas cut me off.

"Where is the man now?" he asked.

"Well, I heard a scream, and a crash, and I ran into the alley to see what had happened, but when I got there, it was empty. "Whoever was there had disappeared!" I explained.

"Disappeared? Really?" Atlas responded, clearly unimpressed.

"I'm telling you the truth, I promise! I don't know what else could have happened!" I said in desperation.

Atlas shook his head in disappointment. He clearly did not believe me.

"I told you not to fail me Thomas," he said.

"But sir, I can still finish my first mission!"

"It's too late for that," Atlas said. "Meet me tomorrow at the office at noon. I'll give you one more chance for another mission. Don't be late."

"I won't." I said quickly.

"Good, go home and get some rest. You'll need it." Atlas said as he abruptly turned and walked out of the alley where we had been talking.

"Why is he like that?" I muttered to myself as I got in the car ready to drive home in darkness.

I checked my watch. It was 10:13 pm. Great, I thought,

Ghost Town

Robert and Mia are probably already asleep. I'm going to have to be super quiet when I go inside. By now, the night had gotten pitch black with low scud clouds. What's worse is halfway through the drive raindrops started to splatter on the car.

Suddenly, the car in front of me stopped moving. I slammed on the brakes, but it was too late. I crashed into the other car. I wasn't hurt, just dazed and confused. Did they run out of gas or something? Why would someone stop randomly in the middle of the road? I got out and went to check if the driver was ok. But when I got there, I found no one was in the driver's seat. Shivers ran down my spine. The car was completely empty.

Shaken—and after looking over the front end of the old gray car I was driving, I slipped back behind the steering wheel and pulled the shift lever into drive. As I made it back to Robert's house, I quietly parked the busted-up car and crept through the front door to the house. I was not pleased to see him waiting for me.

"Where have you been?" asked Robert. "It's past midnight!"

"I got the job," I said unenthusiastically.

"What's with the low face?" he asked me.

"Robert, I blew my first mission. I can't afford to blow

Chapter Four

my second one. My boss told me to meet him at the office at noon tomorrow. He's giving me a second chance."

Robert was taken aback at what I had just said. He seemed at a loss for words.

"Ok, well that's good—maybe next time don't scare us like that. Mia and I were worried. We thought that maybe you . . ."

"Maybe I what?" I interjected angrily remembering the conversation they had about me I had overheard through the walls of the bedroom.

"Never mind," Robert said quickly. "I think we all need some sleep; I'll see you in the morning. Goodnight."

I collapsed onto the bed, dreading tomorrow. So much for a great first day at work. In college Robert used to stay up all night and party, and he procrastinated until the last second to do his work. This new Robert could not have been more different. I just wished I could see my family and not have to do all this. I kept thinking about the thief in the alley and the car crash. Maybe somehow the two events were related.

Chapter Five

The next morning, I could barely get out of bed. I rolled over and pulled the thermal blanket over my head. I didn't feel like I had slept at all last night. I lazily dragged myself away from the comfort of my bed and got up. I did my normal morning routine with little interest. The upcoming meeting with Atlas at his office consumed my thoughts. After Robert and Mia got up, we ate breakfast together with little to no conversation.

"So," Robert finally spoke up after long silence. "Would you like to elaborate on what happened yesterday?" he asked me.

"Well, I got into a car crash." I said. "The car in front of me just randomly stopped and I crashed into them. But then something weird happened. I got out to check if the driver was ok, but no one was in the car."

"What do you mean?" Robert asked concerningly.

Ghost Town

"There's no such thing as a self-driving car."

"*I know*," I said.

A little while later after getting dressed I hopped into the beat-up car and tightly wrapped my fingers around the wheel. It was finally a nice and sunny day, and the clear blue sky seemed to brighten my mood. Today was completely different than last night. I just hoped Atlas would be in a good mood too. I quickly parked the car and headed upstairs to Atlas's office. I was surprised to see that Jerimiah wasn't there. I remembered Elizabeth had said that he was a workaholic. I climbed the stairs to the third floor when I overheard Atlas and Elizabeth talking in his office. I hid behind the wall outside of Atlas's office.

"Elizabeth, think about it." I could hear Atlas say through the walls. "This place is in shambles. We barely make enough money to not go into bankruptcy. We haven't been successful since—well since . . . Elijah." His tough voice softened at that word.

Who was Elijah? I thought.

"What do you say we leave this place together?" Atlas asked Elizabeth.

"You're asking me to leave? What about everyone else? We can't ditch them!" Elizabeth snapped back.

Chapter Five

"I understand." said Atlas, "Now go down to the front desk and see if Thomas is here yet. I need to give him his next mission."

I deliberately waited until Elizabeth had gone down to the front desk before I emerged from behind the wall and knocked on the door to Atlas's office.

"Thanks for being on time, Thomas," said Atlas once he let me into his office. "I'm going to forget about yesterday and give you a second chance for your mission. Besides, Jerimiah needs my help with something, so this needs to be quick."

"Um, Jerimiah's not here." I said.

"What do you mean? I saw him walk in. He talked to me about needing my help. What are you talking about?" Atlas questioned.

"Really?" I asked. "I didn't see him anywhere . . ."

"What?" Atlas rushed out of the room. I decided to follow him since I was the one who brought it up. "Drake, have you seen Jerimiah?" Atlas asked.

"No, I haven't seen him, why?" Drake answered.

"He's probably just left early or something," muttered Atlas.

"You don't . . . you don't think Jerimiah quit, do you?" I asked.

Ghost Town

"No, no he wouldn't quit—not on purpose that is. Something must have happened. He is another one of our all-star detectives." Atlas explained.

"Who's your other all-star detective?" I asked.

"Look, I need you to complete your mission because right now I've got other things to deal with," Atlas told me gruffly, dodging my question. "A police officer reported that one of their best friends went missing. Go investigate the scene. Right now, he's staying in a hotel on Amber Street." Atlas continued.

"Ok . . . I won't let you down this time sir." I answered.

I headed back outside and crawled into the front seat of the car determined not to get distracted this time. As I drove through the backroads, traffic was very heavy. Lines of cars were backed up and I had to take a detour just to make it to the right street. I realized exactly what had gone wrong when I made my final turn. A hotel building was completely on fire. I rolled down my window and heard screams of panic. This was the exact building where I was supposed to be doing detective work in. I swiftly parked the car and got outside to see people panicking. The flames of the building engulfed my eyes. I could hardly see through all the smoke. The fire department had clearly not arrived yet.

Chapter Five

"Help me! My daughter is still in that building!" yelled a woman who looked to be extremely upset.

"Your daughter?" I asked horrified.

"Yes, please! You've got to help me!" pleaded the women. She had long brown hair and was wearing a gray dress.

"What floor is she on?" I asked

"I-I don't know what floor she's on. She's a young girl, only nine years old." said the woman.

"I'll find your daughter," I said, making my decision.

I sprinted into the burning building and immediately became lightheaded due to the lack of oxygen. I quickly realized this was a bad idea. My breathing became heavy and hot. I found the stairs and made my way up to the second floor.

Their daughter must be around here somewhere, I thought to myself.

Getting weaker and weaker I kept going up floor by floor. On floor three a giant piece of wood blocked the stairwell. Determined, I slammed my body against the wood, but it wouldn't budge. Obviously, I needed another plan. I took a breath and realized how hard I was pushing myself. With my body aching I went to look for another route upward. I grabbed some of the debris that wasn't on fire in the stairwell to create a path over the wood barricade

Ghost Town

to climb to the fourth floor. I looked up through the smoke curling in the stairwell and saw a young girl crying for help in the corner. She was stuck on the fifth floor around fifteen feet above me.

"I'm here to help you. What's your name?" I asked the girl. I tried to be as steady as possible with my words.

The girl slowly looked down and saw me. She quietly said, "My name is Lilly, and I want to get out of here."

Seeing no other way for Lilly to get down I said to her, "You're going to get out of here. I'm going to need you to jump. I promise, I will catch you."

"But that's super far down, I . . . I can't jump," Lilly said.

"It's going to be alright. I'm going to catch you. On three—ready? One, two, three!"

Lilly sprang from the floor above me and into my arms. At the same time a deafening crash pierced our ears while dust, and debris filled the air. Lilly tightened her grip around me. My heart was pounding, and I struggled to get a breath of fresh air.

"You, ok?" I asked.

"I'm ok," she said quietly.

"Alright, let's get you out of here," I told her.

Suddenly, a chill went down my spine. I looked at Lilly. Her expression had turned into fear. Her body became

Chapter Five

ghostly white, and a second later she vanished. Panic overtook me. I rubbed my eyes, but she didn't return. My arms were empty! Her hands vanished from where she was holding onto me. I was stunned. This whole thing had to be a dream, right? I pinched myself but nothing happened except the pain due to the pinch.

Just then, pounding footsteps came toward me. I whipped around. It was a firefighter.

"Lilly, she disappeared, I . . ."

"Who is Lily?" The firefighter interrupted. "There's no one else here."

"No!" I yelled. "She was right here and now she's gone!" I could feel myself going pale.

"Okay, that's enough, you're clearly at a loss for oxygen," the firefighter said.

That was the last thing I remembered before I blacked out.

I opened my eyes and glanced at the dark sky above me. What happened? How long had I been lying here? Next to me stood the woman from the street who had asked me to save her daughter. Right behind her stood the firefighter.

"Hold on, let him get his bearings first," said the firefighter.

I got up from the pavement.

Ghost Town

"Wha . . . what . . . happened?" I asked.

"This is Amelia," said the firefighter. "You've been unconscious for around an hour now."

"You ran into the hotel and told me you would find my daughter," said Amelia. She looked very angry but also filled with grief. "What happened to her?"

I was still trying to process where I was when the firefighter said, "You are the only witness. The building is completely destroyed now, but you said you saw her daughter. Tell us what happened."

That's when it all came back to me.

"Yes, I saw her, she told me her name was Lilly. I went into the building and found her, and then—well, then her body turned white, and she vanished right in front of me."

"Vanished? What do you mean? Is she dead?" asked Amelia.

"I don't think your daughter is dead, but I don't think she's alive either." I answered.

Before Amelia could respond to what I said I saw someone walk up to us.

The man looked familiar. Then, I realized who he was.

Amelia then said, "This is my husband, Officer Ashdown."

I wanted to go back to being fainted. Out of all the

Chapter Five

people she could be married to, it had to be a police officer who was out to get me! For a second Ashdown and I glared at each other. Then he yelled at me. "Thomas! Do you know how much trouble you could be in?"

"You know this man?" Amelia asked Ashdown.

"Yes, I know him! Are you kidding? Thomas is the one who drove that train and made headlines. You know, you have a knack for doing things you shouldn't be doing." he said to me.

"More like I have a knack for doing the right thing." I shot back.

"You just added to the problems that we were dealing with during that burning building. You promised my wife you would save our daughter, and look at that, you came out empty-handed." Ashdown framed.

"I tried to save her, but she disappeared! I'm telling you the truth!" I answered.

"You let her die!" Ashdown's words shook me. In the corner I could see Amelia shedding a tear. I suddenly felt very guilty.

"That's enough Officer. I saw the whole thing. He was just trying to do the right thing." said the firefighter.

"Fine I'll let you off this time." Ashdown snapped back.

Officer Ashdown then grabbed me by the shirt and

Ghost Town

lifted me in the air and off my feet. His bulk clearly outmatched mine.

"Don't mess with me or my family ever again. Because next time, I'll mess back." Ashdown stated.

Then he dropped me, and I fell to the hard concrete floor. That's when I realized something.

"Officer Ashdown, you're the police officer who filed a missing case to Atlas." I said bewildered.

"How'd you know that?" he asked me as his eyes turned curious for a second.

I pulled out my badge and showed it to him. It read *Foglight Investigations*.

"Atlas Copper?" I asked. "You know him, don't you?"

"I have no idea what you're talking about," he said as he walked away leaving me there.

Chapter Six

I couldn't get Ashdown's face out of my mind as I drove home. I felt more alone than ever. Am I going crazy? I saw her disappear! Was it just me? I started to think back to the previous events. I had crashed Robert's car into another car with no one driving it. Did the driver disappear in the same way Lily did? With their body turning white? It couldn't be just that girl who disappeared that way. What about the other people? All these unanswered questions pained me. Part of me didn't want to believe what I had seen. The other part did. I felt torn. Eventually, I got back and parked Robert's car in the garage, got out, and opened the door to the house and stepped inside.

"How was work?" Robert asked. "Did your second mission go better than your first one?"

"Robert," I said. "Something weird is going on. This is going to sound bizarre, but during work I went into a burning building to try and save a little girl."

Robert's face shifted between intrigue and disbelief.

"I found her, but then she disappeared right out of my arms—I swear!"

Robert stared at me; his expression now unreadable.

"And that's not all," I said, my tongue loosening up with every word that came next.

"When I crashed your car, the car I crashed into was moving at least forty miles per hour, yet there was no one driving it. How can that be Robert? Or think about the conductor of the train? Isn't it weird that the train was running fine and then suddenly, he was just . . . gone? It's like he vanished out of thin air."

I took a deep breath, my heart racing.

"What I'm trying to say is, I think people are disappearing from this Earth. Go ahead, laugh." I added.

But Robert didn't laugh, he looked at me with a solemn face.

"You can't seriously expect me to believe that. Sure, that might be weird, but those are just coincidences. Yesterday you came home because you crashed my car, and now you're saying you came home because you were trying to save a little girl? Thomas, you've been going hard lately, are you really sure that's what happened?" asked Robert.

Chapter Six

"Yes, she disappeared, I saw her! I would have saved her if not for that! I'm telling you the truth!" I explained.

"Thomas, look at yourself for a second." he said.

Then he left the room leaving me alone. I couldn't believe it! Robert was the only person I thought would believe me. If I couldn't trust him? Who could I trust?

That night I laid in bed all night tossing and turning but never falling asleep. I kept replaying what Robert said to me. *Look at yourself.* I got the feeling that I was back in slavery in ragged clothes working late into the night hours.

Eventually morning came and I dragged myself out of bed. I could tell it was going to be a long day. The cold front from a week ago had come back along with intense fog which darkened the sky outside.

As soon as Robert got up, he came into my bedroom.

"Hey Thomas?" he asked. "I didn't mean what I said to you last night. I'm sorry. I just get the feeling that sometimes you're chasing after something you're never going to find." said Robert.

"Don't worry about it." I said back not wanting any more drama between him and I.

"Oh, by the way," said Robert changing the subject. "The talent show for Emma's school is tonight. You should come. You'd enjoy it more than you'd think."

Ghost Town

"Okay, but first I need to go to work," I said.

I badly wanted to talk to Atlas about last night. I wondered what his connection to Officer Ashdown was, and what he would think about Lily disappearing. After a quick twenty-five-minute drive to Atlas's office, I briskly walked through the doors.

"Elizabeth, where is Atlas? I really need to talk to him." I said.

"Oh," she said sadly. "He's gone."

"What? He's gone? Why? I need him right now!" I stated.

"Well, you and I are the only people here right now. I debated even showing up for work today." Elizabeth said glumly.

"What? Where is everyone?" I asked.

"I think it's time I tell you a little more about Atlas's story." Elizabeth said. "Atlas didn't always act the way he acts nowadays. He used to have a very upbeat and positive personality. He had a family—much like you Thomas. But then tragedy struck as his parents and wife perished during World War II. He and his son were the only ones left. His son's name was Elijah. Atlas decided to train Elijah to become his successor. Day after day they worked vigilantly at solving cases. About a month ago, Atlas thought that Elijah was ready, and he was going to retire

Chapter Six

and give Elijah the position as owner of Foglight Investigations. Atlas felt he had gotten too old for the job, and he had other things he wanted to pursue in life. But that's when Elijah mysteriously disappeared, and after looking into it more, Atlas proclaimed that his one and only son had died. He was devastated. Ever since, he's fallen into a bad depression and now has an alcohol problem."

I was stunned. I looked at Atlas in a whole new way after realizing that all of his family died. He wasn't the aggressor—he was the victim. That's why he got so disturbed when Jermiah wasn't at work. He knew that he had disappeared as well.

"Thomas, did you know that a mere three weeks ago we had a dozen employees? But one by one they have gone missing. And besides me, you are the last one who hasn't disappeared yet."

I didn't know how to respond to Elizabeth. My head was spinning.

"I'm sorry Thomas but you're going to have to find a new job if you want money. This company is finished. There's nothing left here." said Elizabeth as she tore an important document in half.

One question stuck out to me that I wanted to ask Elizbeth while I had the chance.

Ghost Town

"Why didn't you go with Atlas?"

"Excuse me?" she said.

"Why didn't you go with Atlas? You knew this company wasn't going to last and Atlas asked you to leave with him, so why didn't you go with him? He clearly wanted you to go."

Elizibeth sighed. "It's complicated. He and I have worked together for years, but in his current state he's far too emotionally unstable. I truly feel bad for him. I never even got to tell him goodbye."

"He didn't deserve what happened to him." I said passionately.

"No, he didn't." Elizabeth agreed.

"So, I guess this is goodbye for us too?" I said.

"Yeah, I guess it is. I'm glad you found us Thomas." Elizibeth said to me.

I exited through the double doors and walked down the street to where I parked the car. I knew I wasn't going crazy! People *were* disappearing. The real question was why?

Once I drove home and walked into the house I went straight to Robert.

"Hey Robert," I said. "I need to find a new job."

"Why? What happened?" he asked.

"Well, my boss ran away. He was the founder of the com-

Chapter Six

pany, and without him Foglight Investigations shut down."

"Oh, I'm sorry to hear that. Maybe you can find another job in the newspaper." Robert said.

I scrolled through the paper while making myself a quick piece of toast for lunch. The headline read. *Mass cases of people mysteriously vanishing on the spot.*

"See—Robert right here!" I pointed to the headline.

"People are disappearing all around you, and you don't even realize it!" I said.

But Robert seemed disinterested in anything related to the disappearances.

"Oh, by the way Thomas, are you coming tonight? For the talent show?" Robert asked.

I thought about it for a second. Partly because of the fact that I had nothing else to do and partly because I wanted to stay on good terms with Robert, I decided to say yes.

The afternoon blended into the evening and a few hours later we were in the car driving to the talent show. We arrived at the school and made our way to the stage in the auditorium. Robert told me that he and Mia had volunteered to help set up chairs and he asked if I would help. Bright colorful props filled the back of the stage. Standing in the middle of them, I met the director of

Ghost Town

the talent show, whose name was Marcus Pierce. He was dark-skinned, somewhat short, and was very outspoken. One by one the families started to file in while Robert, Mia, and I took our seats in the fourth row from the stage. Approximately thirty minutes later Marcus got up on stage and kicked the event off by introducing the school staff. He seemed very stressed and abruptly walked off stage. The lights dimmed and after a short while he came back on stage.

"Sorry about that," Marcus said. "It appears Mrs. Hailey is running late. I'm sure she will be here any minute. While we wait for her to show up, I want to introduce you to our student council members this year. First up is Oliver Gatlin."

The audience applauded and a tall, blond-haired boy stepped up to the stage. Marcus went down the list naming every kid in student council until there was just one name left.

"And, last but not least we have our student council president, Henry Stevens!" Marcus called out.

The audience applauded but no one came up to the stage. For a second everyone was quiet. I craned my neck and looked to where the other student council members had been standing before they had been called up to the stage.

Chapter Six

"I repeat, Henry Stevens, please come up to the stage." Marcus said as he stood there looking nervous. He looked like he was shaking.

Still, no one came up to the stage. Suddenly, I heard murmuring from the seats behind me. That's when I realized what had happened. Henry had disappeared.

"I assure you all Henry isn't gone; he's probably just in the bathroom or something." Marcus said.

"You're lying." I said. The words came out of my mouth before I even knew what I was doing.

"Henry is gone; he disappeared!" I shouted. I was now standing up in my seat with the whole crowd of people staring at me.

"Thomas, what are you doing?" Robert said somewhat angrily under his breath. "He's not coming back either." I said.

"Excuse me?" Marcus said as he looked bewildered.

Emotions were overtaking me.

"Hold close onto what you have, because it won't last forever." I said.

I stormed out of the auditorium before Marcus could respond to me. I was sick of people not believing me. This was my breaking point. A moment later Robert came behind me. He looked shocked.

Ghost Town

"Thomas, what are you doing? You ruined the show!" he said sharply.

"Let's get out here," I muttered.

The car ride home was shrouded in silence. No one spoke, not even Emma who was usually cheerful and talkative.

Once we got home Emma and Mia rushed upstairs as Robert and I unpacked the trunk of his car and brought leftover props into the house.

"So, are you going to say anything?" Robert asked me.

"What is there to say? I'm telling the truth, people are disappearing. What I said at the talent show was true. And if you won't believe me then that's your loss." I said.

Robert gave me the same expression as before—a kind of sad disappointed one. Then he said, "I'll be right back. I've got to talk to Mia."

Robert walked up the stairs and left me there standing in the kitchen.

"Mia? Emma?" Robert called. "Mia?"

"Thomas, have you seen Emma or Mia?" Robert asked concerningly.

"Last I saw they were going upstairs." I said.

Robert and I suddenly stared blankly at each other. I think we were both thinking the worst. We had seen Mia

Chapter Six

and Emma trek up the stairs no more than five minutes ago. Mia and Emma had disappeared just like the others . . .

Chapter Seven

"Mia?" Robert called louder and louder checking every room of the house. "No! No!"

I was heartbroken at what I was witnessing. I didn't know what to say.

"Thomas get out. Leave my house." Robert said as his voice filled with terror.

"What? What did I do?" I was shocked that he was going this extreme.

"Ever since you showed up problems have started happening."

"What, you think I made them disappear? Robert this is beyond me. I warned you this would happen!"

Robert glared at me, and I saw a tear stream down his cheek.

"I don't care. Just leave my house!" he screamed.

That was the final straw that broke our friendship.

Ghost Town

"Fine," I said as I quickly grabbed my suitcase, keys to the car and jacket and turned for the door.

"You're not the same person I knew ten years ago." I said.

Robert was speechless. And, before he could respond, I pulled the front door shut behind me. I now felt more alone than ever. Part of me sympathized with Robert. He had just lost his whole family. But the other part of me felt angry that he was blaming me for all this. I told him this was going to happen, but he didn't believe me! *Who would believe you?* said a small voice in the back of my mind.

I took the keys and started the engine on the car and drove to the only other place I could think of at the time. The detective company. Where else would I go? I had no money and no home. I just hoped the doors were unlocked. There had to be at least one person there, right? It was late at night and cold. The streets were deserted. Halfway through the drive it started to rain.

I parked the car and walked in the rain towards the narrow building. As I walked, I looked around and realized that there were no shadows. I glanced up at the streetlight above me. It was out. I looked up and down the street and realized they were all out. Not only that, all the windows in the buildings on both sides of the street where I stood were dark as well. Must be a blackout, I thought.

Chapter Seven

I walked up to the building and entered through the door to the detective company. Thankfully, the doors were unlocked. It was just as dark inside the building as outside. I stumbled my way around the dark lobby where I could see a small flicker of light coming from the second story. I made my way up the stairs and found several candles set on tables. Suddenly, I heard someone crying. It was coming from Atlas's office. I climbed up the stairs to the third story, opened the big office door, and saw Atlas on the floor crying in the middle of the room. Bottles of red wine had spilled everywhere on the floor. A single candle was set on the bookcase which partially lit the room.

"Atlas?" I asked. "What's going on?"

"They all disappeared. Everyone—even Elizabeth." he said quietly.

"I thought you left?" I asked.

"I came back Thomas. I felt bad about leaving. But when I got back, no one was there." Atlas explained.

"Elizabeth might not have disappeared." I said, trying to cheer him up. "She said she was leaving the company when you left." She may still be out there somewhere. And maybe some of the others are still out there too." I lied.

My words didn't seem to help. Atlas sat up and picked

up another wine bottle and began to drink it.

"Atlas? How many bottles of wine have you had?" I asked.

"They're all gone Thomas. You're going to be next." Atlas said.

Atlas started crying again and muttered the words *Elijah* under his breath.

"You know I have a son." I said as I sat down next to him. "I don't know if he's still even out there. I lost some valuable time with him."

A sudden feeling of bittersweetness filled me.

"I used to do everything with him. He was such a happy kid. But he's no longer a kid anymore." I said as a single tear rolled down my face. I know how it feels to lose family. It feels like there's nothing else that the world has to offer. You feel . . ."

"Empty?" Atlas said as he wiped a tear from his own face.

"Yeah," I said sadly.

Suddenly, I heard a loud noise coming from downstairs. Someone else had entered the building. I had a very bad feeling.

"But I'm hopeful things will change. Let's get out of here." I told Atlas quickly.

I stood up and extended my hand for Atlas to grab,

Chapter Seven

but his body abruptly turned ghostly white—almost transparent just like Lilly's had done right before my eyes. A few seconds later, he disappeared into thin air.

I fell onto the floor not believing what I had just witnessed. I put my hands on the spot where he was sitting just seconds ago. I'm sure red wine was all over my hands and jacket, but I didn't care.

"No! Nooooo!" I yelled. "Why is this happening? Atlas didn't deserve what happened to him!"

Just as I was processing Atlas's disappearance, someone burst open the large brown door into his office.

"Freeze!" The person yelled.

I whipped around and saw Officer Ashdown standing in the middle of the doorway looking at me dumbfounded.

"Thomas? What did you do to him?" Ashdown said horrified, as he looked at the red wine dripping from my hands and jacket.

I panicked. Not him again! How did Ashdown even find me? I immediately tried to run out from the door, but Ashdown grabbed me and cuffed my arms behind my back, and pinned me against the wall.

"I told you I would mess back," he muttered. "What did you do to him?"

Ghost Town

"I didn't do anything to him. Atlas disappeared right in front of me!" I pleaded.

"Atlas? How do you know Atlas?" Ashdown asked.

"I already told you. I worked for him. For *Foglight Investigations*." I said.

"I don't trust you. Everywhere you go people disappear. First the train, then the burning building and now I hear that you disrupted a whole talent show!" Ashdown said.

"I didn't mean for any of this to happen. I just wanted to find my wife and son!" I said.

"Your family is probably already gone. You do know that right?" Ashdown sneered.

His words broke my heart. I had come to accept that they might not be alive, but hearing Ashdown say it just made it hurt on another level. I started thrashing to try and get unpinned from the wall, but he was too strong, and I was subdued.

"Your debt from the train is due in three weeks. But seeing as you're definitely not getting the money, I think I should just go ahead and take you to jail."

"What? But I haven't done anything wrong!"

"I think you've caused more than enough trouble," said Ashdown.

Ashdown directed me out of the detective building

Chapter Seven

and into his police car. He chained my handcuffs to the police car and started driving away. My stomach churned as I saw the last glimpse of the detective building. Things were not looking up.

Chapter Eight

One moment I was grieving over Atlas, and the next moment I was in jail. Once we arrived, Ashdown directed me out of the car and took me inside.

"Where are the other prisoners?" Ashdown asked as he looked at the empty cells of the jailhouse.

"They vanished," said a guard in the room. He was a strong framed blond-haired man. I read the nametag on his uniform. It read *Daniel Raven*.

"There's no trace of them escaping. I don't know what happened!" said Daniel.

Ashdown glared at me like I had just murdered someone.

"Put this one in place of them." he said as he gave me a nudge towards Daniel.

There was no point resisting as my hands were handcuffed and there was no way for me to escape. Daniel

Ghost Town

took me by the handcuffs and directed me into a cell. He pulled the door shut, and just like that I was imprisoned.

Ashdown and Daniel were still in the hallway outside my cell, so I peered out from my bars to try and listen to what they were saying.

"This is the man who crashed the train into those buildings?" asked Daniel.

"Yep, and something's up with him. I think he is making people disappear. Have you heard the news lately? Mass cases of people are disappearing without a trace!" stated Ashdown.

"I'm not making people disappear!" I yelled as I began to feel felt hot-headed.

"Well, then maybe you'll disappear yourself." Ashdown snickered. "Let's go somewhere more private to talk." he told Daniel.

Ashdown and Daniel left the hallway outside my cell, leaving me all alone. It was just me and my thoughts. A single dim light bulb lit up my cell. I should have had cell mates, but it seemed they had disappeared. I was in a windowless, clockless cell.

I began to wonder if Ashdown was right. Was I making people disappear? If I was—I certainly wasn't doing it on purpose. Although, he did have a point, because

Chapter Eight

everywhere I went people disappeared.

Two whole days passed as I lay in my cell. Every once in a while, during the day Daniel would come in and slip my meals through the bars. This is torturous! I thought. I tried escaping but there was no feasible method out. I tried prying the bars open, tried pleading to Daniel, but it was all useless.

For another two days I sat miserably with my back against the cold concrete wall of the cell awaiting any human interaction. I glanced in the mirror hanging above the sink. I looked at my face and saw dark circles forming under my eyes. I thought back to four days ago when I had left Robert and watched Atlas disappear. Grief washed over me. I wondered if Robert was still here or if he had disappeared as well. Later that day Daniel came to deliver me food. I pleaded with him to let me go.

"Please! You've got to let me out of here!" I begged.

"I'm sorry but it's Ashdown's orders to keep you in here," Daniel explained.

"Ashdown is wrong! He falsely imprisoned me." I shouted.

"I'm not letting you out." Daniel said bluntly. Then he exited the hallway leaving me alone again.

I sighed and sank lower to the floor. My energy was

fading. I spent what felt like hours trying to think of the best thing to say to Daniel to get him to release me when he came back to deliver me food. But my mind felt blank as my hunger increased. I eventually thought of telling him that yes, I had the power to make people disappear and I was the one behind everyone vanishing. I would then threaten him that if they didn't comply to let me out, I would make them disappear. Ashdown knows people are vanishing, but he's not doing anything about it. The plan wasn't very good. But it was my only chance of getting out of here.

So, I waited. And waited. I expected Daniel to show up any minute to deliver me a meal. But as more time passed, he didn't show up. I began to get suspicious. My stomach churned from hunger. *He should have shown up by now*, I thought.

Then I had a sudden realization. Daniel wasn't coming back. He had disappeared. That's why he hadn't come back yet to give me another meal. *Oh no*, I thought. I'm going to die of hunger in this cell. No one will even know I'm dead. There must be a way out of here, I thought. My plan was to convince Daniel to release me, but he was gone now, and he had the key to my cell. I could try and pry the bars, even though I knew that wasn't going

Chapter Eight

to work because I had tried it multiple times earlier. My hunger grew worse as all I could think about was a fresh meal. Don't panic, I told myself. Besides, you've got at least another week or two before you truly starve to death. That's enough time to get out, right? But soon enough I realized there was no escape. I was not going to die heroically or tragically; I was going to die in the most pitiful way possible. I tried to sleep as much as possible so I wouldn't feel the pain of hunger in my sleep. But I couldn't sleep forever, and on the seventh day, I fell to the floor in pain. Then out of nowhere, the door opened.

"Daniel?" I managed to croak.

I was so weak and limp I could barely get myself up from the floor. As the man stepped into the room outside my cell. I realized who it was—It was Robert! He stepped forward towards my cell and tossed me a newspaper.

"You were right," he muttered.

I read the front cover of the newspaper. It read; "*Mass cases of people disappearing without a trace.*" I didn't feel the need to read any further. Suddenly my stomach groaned, and I fell back to the floor.

"I figured you were starving so I brought you a ham sandwich and a cup of coffee." Robert said.

At the mention of food, I became hyper-aware. I

devoured the sandwich and drank delicious sips of the coffee. Food reinvigorated me. My brain suddenly started to work again.

"How did you find me?" I asked.

"Thomas, you're practically famous. You were right. About everything. This is all my fault. It could have been prevented if I didn't get so angry." Robert said as he hung his head.

"It's not your fault," I interrupted. "And I don't know whose fault it is either."

"It's just that now I know what it's like to lose a wife and a child. They were only gone for five seconds, and I couldn't control my anger. I couldn't imagine what it would be like not seeing my family for ten years. I'm sorry for what I said to you. I was filled with grief." Robert said.

"I'm not going to hold a grudge," I said.

"Ok then, let's go," said Robert.

"Go where?" I asked.

The truth was I felt like there was nowhere left to go.

"To go find your family, of course," Robert said.

"My family's gone." I said. "I accepted that a long time ago. They probably disappeared, and we have no idea if they would still be living in the same house."

"Well, you found me living in the same house, so

Chapter Eight

chances are you'll find your family. Sometimes you need to listen to your own advice. You said you would rather die than lose your family again. Would you rather rot in this cell and disappear or disappear with your family? Besides, I've got nothing left to lose." explained Robert.

"Yeah, but how am I going to get out of here?" I asked.

"Don't worry about it," Robert said as he took a key out of his pocket.

"How did you find the key to my cell?" I asked.

"It was right where the guard left it."

"Ok, let's get out of here," I said, filled with hope.

We snuck out the doors of the jail. The entire jail was empty. It seemed that everyone guarding it had disappeared.

"So, we are going to drive all the way from Virginia to California?" I asked. "Are you sure about this?"

"Correct," said Robert. "We can take turns driving and we can stop at a few hotels to sleep. It should take us three days. It'll be fine. Trust me."

"Ok, let's go." I said.

When I first met back up with Robert in his beach house, I didn't think he would be putting in this much effort for me. This reminded me of the way Robert used to be. A more go with the flow kind of person. But it's good that he changed, I reminded myself. Embracing change is how we become the best versions of ourselves. So, as Robert drove, I explained everything all the way back to the burning building. This time he believed me. I told him about Atlas's disappearing and Officer Ashdown taking me to jail. Robert told me that in the seven days that I had spent in jail, chaos was ensuing in the world. More and more people were vanishing out of thin air and by now, it was a worldwide phenomenon.

"Where do you think the people go when they disappear?" Robert asked me.

"I . . . I don't know . . ." I answered.

That night, we stopped at a hotel to sleep and got up early to continue the drive. The hotel was lit by candles since there was now some type of power outage caused by many workers at the power company disappearing. Back on the road we saw many empty cars and crashes—likely due to people who were driving them and then disappeared. I was worried about my family, but I tried to remain as hopeful as possible.

The next night was more of the same as the first, with Robert and I stopping at a hotel. We drove the whole third day and we were getting close to my family's old neighborhood.

Chapter Eight

"Robert," I said, asking a question that had been on my mind for a while. "What's going to happen if one of us disappears?"

"Well, I would think that whoever doesn't disappear would just keep going. I mean, there's not much else to do." he said.

"I guess . . . I mean who would do this? Make people disappear? For fun? I just don't understand. Robert!" I screamed suddenly. "Brake! There's a car stopped in front of us, don't you see it?"

That's when I glanced over at Robert and realized he was not driving the car. His body was a misty transparent white, and a second later, he disappeared.

Robert's truck collided with the other car, but I was too stunned to care. I couldn't believe it. Not Robert, he was my closest friend aside from my wife. What kind of twisted person would do this?

"Robert? Robert?" I called, pleading that he would magically reappear. But no one was there. I was alone.

I thought back to the last words Robert spoke to me. *I think whoever doesn't disappear should just keep going. I mean there's not much else to do*, he had said. Keep going. I took those words to heart. There was still hope that I could see my family before I died, or whatever would happen to me if I disappeared. A part of me wondered why I hadn't disappeared yet. I had watched practically everyone around me vanish, so why not me?

I unfastened my seatbelt and crawled out of the wreckage. I decided I was going to continue on foot—knowing that my family's house was only a few miles from here. The streets were deserted. A usually bustling city had now become a ghost town.

I reached my neighborhood and walked up to my old house. I still remembered the house vividly. The blue siding with the white roof was simply too iconic to forget. With a heavy heart I rang the doorbell. I waited with bated breath as someone opened the door. It was Olivia! Relief filled my heart. She wasn't gone after all!

In disbelief Olivia stammered. "T . . . Thomas?" She looked at me for a second like I was a stranger. "Is that really you? You're . . . you're here? After all this time?"

"Yes," I said, finally drawing breath. "It's me."

For a second Olivia kept looking at me. Then she threw her arms around me and burst into tears.

"I'm here," I said reassuring her.

I was overjoyed to be reunited with my family. I just had to see Issac.

"Is Issac here?" I asked.

"Yes, he's here, he's upstairs in his room. He's probably

Chapter Eight

asleep but I'm sure he is going to want to see you." Olivia exclaimed.

"It's been too long," I stammered. "I'm sorry, I should have come earlier. And now everyone is disappearing and I . . . I thought that you had already disappeared. I have been trying to get here but it has been so hard!"

"At least you're here now," Olivia said. "It's been so difficult raising Issac without you in our lives."

"We're all together now," I reassured her.

I walked upstairs and approached the door to Issac's room. It still blew my mind to think that Issac was now a teenager. When I had last been with him, he had been a toddler. I opened the door but there was no one in the room. I pulled the blanket off the bed. There was no one there. Panic erupted in my head.

"Olivia, he's not up here!" I yelled. No response. "Olivia?" I called again. Still no response.

I flew down the stairs but there was no one there.

"Olivia, this isn't funny, please answer me! Issac? Olivia? Anyone?"

"No!" I stammered. "Not like this!"

But, sure enough, in the spot Olivia had been standing a minute ago, there was now no one. My family had disappeared.

Chapter Nine

I was in disbelief. No, they couldn't be gone. I had to be imagining things. I mean things were finally looking up for me. I didn't care if anyone else disappeared. Just a moment ago I was happy to be with my family again. To be with Olivia, to be with Issac, to finally have the opportunity to play a simple game of catch with my only son; all of that was now gone. I fell to the floor in tears.

Ashdown was right. Every person I encountered disappeared. The train conductor, Atlas, Ashdown's family, Robert's family and now my own family. How could I let this happen? I finally had gotten to see them after ten years and then they just got ripped away from me. I felt like I had nowhere left to go. I got up and stormed out of the house full of anger. I didn't know where I was going but I bolted from the porch and started running down the street. I didn't look back. That's when I heard a familiar voice.

Ghost Town

"Freeze!" someone shouted from behind me.

I turned around and saw Officer Ashdown pointing a gun straight at me. Not him again! I thought. Why couldn't he have disappeared? He deserved to disappear far more than my family did. They did nothing wrong! This is all his fault! If he hadn't put me in jail, I could've seen my family for longer—long enough for me to at least tell them a proper goodbye.

"So, what happened Thomas, did your family disappear?" Ashdown mocked as if he could read my mind. My family disappeared too. But I didn't run away, I did something about it!"

At that moment I wanted to punch Ashdown straight in the face. But I didn't. I steadied myself and decided the best option would be to run. I took one step and Ashdown interrupted; "You move, and I shoot you."

I turned around and froze. I put my hands in the air. "Look, Ashdown, I don't want any trouble. I just—I just want . . ." my voice trailed off.

The truth was I didn't know what I wanted anymore. I had lost my family. The only thing that kept me going.

"You're making people disappear. I know you are. You're the one behind this chaos." Ashdown said. As he spoke drops of light rain came down from above.

Chapter Nine

"For the last time I'm not making people disappear!" I yelled.

"Your lies won't save you this time." Ashdown muttered.

He tightened his grip around the trigger of his gun, but suddenly the gun dropped out of his hand and onto the ground. Ashdown screamed and I looked over at his hand which had become ghostly white and transparent. I don't think I'd ever seen anyone as afraid as Ashdown was at that moment. He looked at me with what seemed to be genuine fear. His voice quaking, he stammered, "What are you doing to me? Whatever you're doing to me, cut it out! I won't hurt you I promise!" he trailed off.

"I'm—I'm . . . not doing anything!" I said.

But a second later Ashdown's entire body became transparent and ghostly white, and then he vanished. I paused for a second and caught my breath. I was still trying to process what had just happened. *He's gone;* I muttered to myself. What now?

From somewhere behind me, I heard what sounded like several people screaming. They started to run in my direction.

"What's happening? Why are you all running?" I asked as they approached me.

Ghost Town

The tall blond-haired man at the front of the group didn't speak but simply pointed behind him. That's when I saw what he was running from—a giant, swirling storm cloud. What looked like a tornado mixed with a hurricane was heading straight towards us. This storm looked different than any normal storm. Pitch black storm clouds engulfed the sky and everything they touched became engulfed into total darkness. Heavy rain poured down from above.

"Anyone who gets swept up by that storm disappears," shouted the man through the raging wind.

He took off running after the rest of the group and I realized I should follow him to save myself. What is that thing? I thought. Is that what's making people disappear?

We raced down the streets of my old neighborhood and eventually came to a split path that veered both right and left. The group chose to go right.

"The exit to the neighborhood is left!" I shouted to the blond-haired man. "That way is a dead end!"

The blond-haired man looked back at me. For a second he hesitated, then he decided to listen, and he started running to the left. We ran out of the neighborhood together and came to the main road.

"Come on! There are miles of roads this way that go

Chapter Nine

by open grassland!" I gestured to the blond-haired man.

That was the thing I liked about my old neighborhood. On one side you were close to the city and on the other you were close to wide open grasslands in the country.

"It's getting closer!" The blond-haired man yelled.

The storm seemed to be moving quicker and quicker. I looked behind me and we watched the storm as it drifted along the sky and passed a pasture. In an instant all the cows who had been peacefully grazing in the pasture suddenly turned ghostly white and then disappeared.

I shuddered in fear. *It's making animals disappear too.* I thought.

Me and the blond-haired man split up. He decided to run one way, and I decided to run the other way. I raced along roads that passed by grasslands. I didn't know if I was going to be able to outrun the storm. Gasping for air, I tripped and fell onto the wet concrete. Rain gushed down from the sky. My clothes were drenched.

"Get up!" I muttered under my breath.

I felt weak and as I picked myself up, I paused. I looked back as I saw the towering storm. I can't outrun this thing forever, I confessed to myself. I don't want my last moments to be in fear. I decided that I was going to go into the storm. Maybe I would see my family after I

Ghost Town

disappeared. There was nothing left for me to do here. Everyone else had already disappeared. Now it was my turn. I stepped forward as the storm was mere yards away from me.

"Goodbye Earth," I said as I stepped into it.

The storm engulfed my body turning it ghostly white and almost completely transparent. A moment later, I disappeared.

I woke up lying on what I thought was a cloud. My vision was dizzy as I stood up. Thankfully, my body was still intact. Where was I? I looked around. I was in a giant circle and gray clouds surrounded the area outside the circle. I couldn't make out anything in the white haze.

"Hello?" I called. "Hello? Is anyone there?" My voice echoed although I wasn't entirely sure how. Suddenly a man stepped into my line of sight. He was thin and had brown hair. He reminded me of Daniel the guard. As I looked at him, I realized that his right arm was missing.

"Who are you?" I asked.

"My name is Easton," he said.

"Where am I? Is this the afterlife? Where is everybody else who disappeared?" I asked while my mind spun with questions.

"Relax," Easton said. "You're in a place called The

Chapter Nine

Mist. And no, this isn't the afterlife. You know that storm you walked into? You're inside of it right now. Time doesn't pass here. You'll get used to it."

"Where is everyone else? I'm not the only one who was engulfed by the storm."

"They're over there." Easton said as he pointed towards a crowd of people I tried to make out in the haze.

I didn't recognize most of the people in the crowd, but there was one I did—Olivia! I ran towards her but bumped into something. An invisible wall prevented me from getting to her. I banged my fists on the invisible wall but nothing happened except pain echoing from my wrists.

"Olivia!" I called out.

There was no response. I looked around at the other people behind her. They seemed to be walking around looking confused. They didn't look like they were in control of themselves.

"She doesn't know you're here. She's on the other side of The Mist along with everyone else who has disappeared. You can see her, but she can't see you." Easton said.

"What do you mean? Why am I on this side while everyone else is on that side of this place?"

"I already told you; you are in The Mist. I was a scientist on Earth and I was trying to find a place outside

Ghost Town

of time. I did several experiments and eventually found this place. I call it The Mist. Time doesn't pass here. You might be wondering why I only have one arm. That's because in one of my experiments I accidentally sent only my right arm into The Mist and not the rest of my body, so I lost an arm. But that didn't stop me, as I kept going until I created a way to get into this place. My experiment went wrong and one by one everybody began to disappear on Earth. Everyone who disappeared ended up here. The reason you're on this side of The Mist is because you chose to disappear. They didn't."

"You did this?" I asked. I was furious.

"I never wanted any of this to happen. I . . . I didn't know." Easton stammered.

But I didn't care if this was an accident. When I considered the amount of pain he had caused me I tried to punch him in the face. My hand went right through his body like I was punching the air.

"Our bodies aren't physical here like on Earth. You can't touch me, and I can't touch you. You may not like it, but I can offer a solution. I have enough technology to send—say... you and five other people back down to Earth. No more storm. No more disappearances. Think about it." Easton said.

Chapter Nine

I paused. *Should I take the deal?* Part of me wanted to. I mean, I knew the exact five people who I would want to send back with me, Robert, Mia, Emma, Olivia, and Issac. I would be able to see and be with all of them again.

"I know who you are, Thomas. I know that all you really want is to see your family. I'm giving you that option." Easton said.

I thought about how many more memories I could make with my family if I took the deal. *No! I told myself.* You're being selfish. Think about all the other people who disappeared? They deserve just as much as I do to return to earth. What about Atlas? What about Elizabeth? Heck, even Ashdown deserved a second chance.

"No." I said to Easton. "I'm not taking the deal. I want everyone to come back—good and bad. I don't care what they did, but they deserve to come back to Earth and not stay up here in this . . ." I cut myself off. I almost said prison.

I looked around at the thousands of people behind the invisible wall. The crowd seemed to stretch forever. Sure, the people were here, but they didn't quite look real.

"Tough one to please, huh? I thought that I was giving you what you wanted." Easton said.

"Is there any way everyone can come back?" I asked.

"No," Easton said. "I'm giving you the only option. You

Ghost Town

can either return to Earth with your family and friends or you can stay here, on the dark side of The Mist."

"Why, do you not want me here?" I asked.

"I never said what I wanted. I only said what you wanted." Easton answered.

"How do you know who I am anyway?" I asked.

"Long story," he said.

"Go on, you can tell it. I'm going to be here for a while because I'm not taking that deal."

Easton looked at me as if I was making the wrong decision.

"Ok, so I . . ."

"What's that?" I interrupted him. Something had caught my attention. I pointed to an old green steering wheel. It was covered with rust and looked as if it belonged on some kind of pirate ship. I thought I recognized it from somewhere.

"Oh that? That's just a ship's wheel that accidentally ended up here due to the experiment." Easton said.

I walked closer to the rusted steering wheel.

"But why is it here? The only thing I've seen here are us and people on the other side of that invisible wall." I said.

"I told you. It ended up here because of an experiment. Just leave it alone and don't touch it." said Easton.

Chapter Nine

"Touch it?" I asked. "I thought you said nothing was physical here."

Easton appeared to bite his lip. I walked slightly closer to the wheel. I knew this wasn't just any ordinary ship's wheel.

"You really don't have to touch it, trust me, it's nothing I promise!" Easton repeated.

"Come any closer and I'll put my hand on it!" I yelled.

Easton stepped back a few feet from the wheel.

"I'm warning you," he said. "If I were you, I wouldn't touch that."

I inched my hand closer to the wheel.

"Ok stop!" he yelled. "Thirty people! I'll send thirty people back down to Earth with you. You'll be with your family again."

"I thought you said you only had the technology to send five people. You lied." I snapped back at him.

"Ok, just stop! I can send everyone back." Easton said.

After hearing that, I withdrew my hands and moved them away from the wheel.

"I lied. The way I lost my arm wasn't through experimentation." Easton admitted. "I turned that wheel to put everyone into The Mist. It nearly killed me. That's how I lost my arm. If you turn that wheel the pain will be so bad you will want to give up. I can send everyone back without you having to lose an arm."

"So, this wasn't an accident?" I shouted. "Do you realize how much pain you caused me? I think you expected me to be just like everyone else and show up on the other side of The Mist, didn't you? So that you would be in control."

"No, that's not what happened, I'm telling you!" Easton muttered.

But it was too late. I laid my hands on the wheel and began turning it to the right. An intense burning sensation filled my arms. I groaned out in pain. It felt like my right arm was being burned alive.

"You'll die before you can fully turn the wheel," Easton said out of breath.

My arms strained in shearing pain as I continued turning the wheel. But I was ready to sacrifice my arm if it meant sending everyone back to earth. The wheel was around one third of the way turned. That's when I heard a loud wind rustling around me. I screamed in pain. I was going to turn this wheel— whatever it took.

As I approached the one hundred-eighty degrees mark of turning the wheel I suddenly heard a deafening crash. I could barely pay attention to anything except the

Chapter Nine

pain—now radiating from both of my arms, but I began to hear people shouting.

"What's happening? Where are we?" asked the people.

The wind roared around me. The pain was now becoming unbearable. I looked ahead as I saw the clouds separate in a flurry of wind. I groaned once more in agony. I was almost there. My right arm had gone numb by this point, but I was able to see people on the other side of the invisible wall turning white and evaporating. I'm getting close, I thought. Someone suddenly approached me from the other side of the wall. For a second, I didn't recognize who it was—then I knew.

"Dad?" the boy asked.

It was Issac, but he was a teenager now, appearing to be at least sixteen years old.

"It's going to be okay Dad, just keep going, don't give up." Issac said.

A moment later I saw Issac vanish and I was all alone. Even Easton had disappeared.

"I'm so close!" I muttered.

But my arm was dying in pain. I tried not to panic but deep red and blue scars began covering my entire right arm and even onto my left arm. I summoned all my strength and turned the wheel a full three hundred-sixty degrees. The clouds had now fully separated, and I looked down at myself. My body had turned ghostly white and a moment later, I disappeared.

I awoke and realized I was back on Earth. I was in the same place I disappeared from—on the streets next to the pasture. I looked over and all the cows were now back. The atmosphere was completely different than before I went into The Mist. It was now a bright sunny day and there was no storm or darkness. People were all scattered around the streets. They were stumbling around and looking totally confused as to what had happened.

"It worked." I said weakly to myself.

My arm still throbbed in pain, but I didn't really care anymore. Everyone was back. There was only one more place left to go. I ran back through the streets towards my old neighborhood. As I ran, I heard people asking questions like; "What happened? Where are we?" They appeared to have no idea what had happened. I don't think they were in control of themselves when they were in The Mist. I finally arrived back at my old house and this time I didn't bother to ring the doorbell. I flung the door open and stepped inside. I saw Olivia and we embraced. I realized just how close I was to almost losing my family again. I headed upstairs and opened the door

Chapter Nine

to Issac's room. I found him lying on his bed.

"Issac!" I said, overwhelmed with joy. I gave him a big hug.

"I love you dad," he said to me as we hugged.

"I love you too son," I said. I was so happy to be reunited with my family—for real this time.

Things only got better from there. The next few weeks were some of the best of my life. I got to finally catch up with my family and share some of the things I had learned. I had so much knowledge and was not the same man I was ten years ago. I told them about the storm, and the people disappearing, and me turning the wheel to bring everyone back to Earth. To most of the world, no one knew what had happened. They didn't know what the storm was, and they didn't know how they got back. Of course, chaos ensued for a while until everyone could figure out where they lived, and could get their lives back to some sense of normalcy. But overall, the world was starting to get itself back on track. And now, I knew I was truly free.

It seemed it wasn't just me who felt like things were going well. Atlas was cheerier than ever as I talked with him over the telephone. Elijah had come back and helped Atlas reopen his detective company and expand into

Ghost Town

a new building that was much nicer and less gloomy. Robert was also happier now that Mia and Emma were back. He apologized again how he had treated me in the past, and even though I had long since forgiven him, our long-time friendship was renewed as we found a new appreciation for each other. I told Robert everything that I told my family, and he thanked me for risking my life to save everyone. My arm was healing slowly everyday as I became healthier. One thing I did realize is that I needed a new job. Robert proposed the idea of us working together where we could go out into the world and free others from slavery, so that no one had to endure what I had to go through.

About a month later Robert's truck pulled into my front driveway while I was in our yard with Issac playing catch. We both walked up to the front porch where we saw Olivia.

"Ok, I've got to go." I said to her.

"Don't ever leave me like you did again." she said.

"I won't. I'll only be gone for a week. Besides, I'll always come back. That's a promise." I said.

I saw the golden sun set as I looked out from my front porch. The once desolate neighborhood that had become a complete ghost town was now bustling with people.

Chapter Nine

Robert got out of his truck and came up to Olivia and I on the porch.

"You ready to leave?" he asked.

"Yeah, I'm ready." I said.

I hugged Issac and Olivia and then walked towards Robert's truck with him.

Suddenly, Olivia called my name.

"Thomas!" she shouted. "The phone is ringing. It's for you!"

I walked back up the porch and into the house. I picked up the phone sitting on the end table in the living room and held the receiver to my ear.

"Hello?" I asked.

"Thomas? Is that you?" asked a familiar voice.

"Yes, it's me, who is this?" I asked.

"It's Atlas. There's a man acting crazy here in my office who says he knows you. He's missing an arm, and he says his name is Easton. He carried this old looking green pirate ship wheel in with him."

I glanced away from the phone and looked at Robert and Olivia, who by then had come into the living room and were standing next to me. I could sense they were thinking the same thing I was thinking. It looked like it was time to solve another mystery.

About The Author

Noah Lane is a first-time author from Davidson, North Carolina, whose passion for writing ignited at a young age. As a natural storyteller, he loves reading and writing about action, adventure, and mystery genres. Noah is also a musician, a former band member of *Picnic at the Costco*, and a guitarist. Outside of his creative endeavors, Noah stays active by playing soccer and mountain biking, always seeking new adventures and challenges. He plans to continue his journey as an author and hopes to publish more books in the future.

www.ingramcontent.com/pod-product-compliance
Lightning Source LLC
LaVergne TN
LVHW041533070526
838199LV00046B/1656